MILKMAN BILL

By JESSICA POTTER BRODERICK

Illustrated by JEAN TAMBURINE

RAND McNALLY & COMPANY
Chicago
Established 1856

Wrapped snugly in a woolly bathrobe, Dickie sat in his mommy's sunny kitchen. It was the first time Dickie had come downstairs after being in bed for a long while, ever since they had moved into the new house three weeks before.

"Dickie, we'll have to wait for Milkman Bill this morning," said Mommy.

Milkman Bill! Dickie had *heard* Milkman Bill. All the while he was in bed, at exactly the same time every morning, Dickie had heard the chugging of the milk truck outside and the cheery jangle of the bottles. Now he was going to *see* Milkman Bill!

Mommy looked out the window.
Then she opened the door. "Come in,
Milkman Bill," she said.

The milkman was jolly, with rosy
cheeks and kind, twinkling eyes.
"Dr. John says Dickie must drink
more milk now," said Mommy.
"We'll need another quart every day."

"Gee," said Dickie. "Can you get all
that extra milk out of your cows,
Milkman Bill?"

"I have no cows," laughed Milkman Bill. "But the *farmers* have cows."

"Then you don't milk any cows at all?"

"No, and the farmers don't either these days, not the ones we deal with

anyway. They use mechanical milkers. They call it Pipeline Milking. The milk flows through a narrow tube from the cow into a strainer. From the strainer it runs through a pipe into a big storage tank. Well, I'd better get along." And Milkman Bill was out the door.

The next morning Dickie had another question for Milkman Bill. "Milkman Bill, what do they do with the milk in the storage tanks?"

"Huge tank trucks come for it. They take it to the big Dairy. That's where I get it. Then I bring it to you."

"That must take a lot of time, getting the milk from the farm to the Dairy and then to me."

"Sometimes only twenty-four hours," said Milkman Bill. "Never more than two days. Well, there's your milk, young fellow. I'd better get along."

Dickie was growing stronger fast. The next morning he got dressed, came downstairs and stood by the kitchen door, waiting for Milkman Bill. But he was late. "I wonder what's the matter?" Dickie asked his mother.

Just then there was a knock at the door and Milkman Bill came in. "Wanted to see how Dickie was," he said, glancing about the room.

"Boo !" shouted Dickie, as he jumped out from behind the door.

"Well, well. Look at those rosy

cheeks. Just shows what milk will do."

"Milkman Bill," said Dickie. "May I ask you *one* more question?"

"Sure, Dickie."

"Did you have a hard time filling the bottles this morning? Spill a lot of milk or something? You're late."

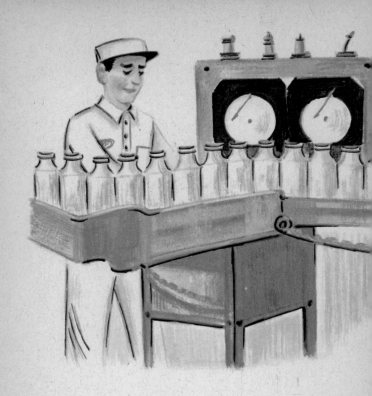

Milkman Bill threw back his head
and laughter filled the room. "A big
machine does it. It takes those
bottles, fills them with milk, then caps
them and seals them.

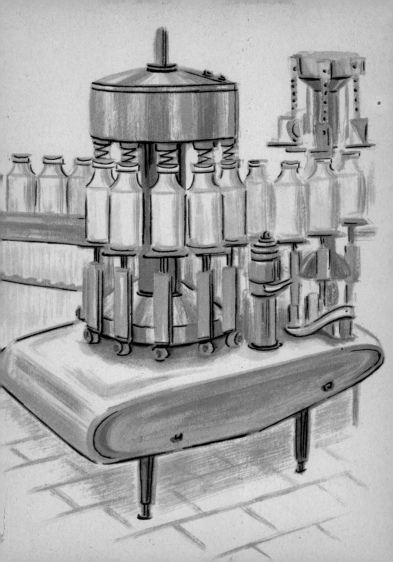

"There are other machines too.
There's the Separator. It separates the
cream from the milk. According to
how you set it, the Separator turns
out whipping cream, table cream,

whole milk, skim milk. There's also a machine that makes butter, another that makes cheese and another that makes ice cream.

"And there's one very important machine called the Pasteurizer. It makes the milk so hot all the germs are killed. Then the milk is safe for boys and girls to drink."

"My, those machines do a lot of work," said Dickie.

"Yes, and when their work is done, ours begins. We load all those good things into our trucks and bring them to you. Well, I'd better get along."

The next morning Dickie could
hardly wait for Milkman Bill to come.
He had something special to tell him.

The milkman was barely inside the door before Dickie was saying, "I'm going to school tomorrow! Dr. John said I might."

"Well, now, that's fine," said Milk-man Bill. "And *I* have a surprise for *you*, Dickie. How would you like to make a tour of the Dairy? The manager said I could take you through next Saturday."

Dickie jumped up and down. "Oh boy!" he squealed. "That would be nice, Milkman Bill."

"Well, I'd better get along. See you—no, I *won't* see you tomorrow, Dickie. You'll be at school. But don't you worry, I'll leave your milk for you every day. And I'll see you on Saturday."

Dickie watched Milkman Bill run down the walk and climb into his truck. "I like Milkman Bill," he said. "I guess he's one of the nicest friends I have."